BELONGING STREET

Poems and Illustrations by
MANDY COE

Otter-Barry BOOKS

CONTENTS

YOU ARE HERE

In the car park is a map of your town.
Everyone presses their finger
on the red dot that says,
You are here.

And here you are!
Inside your shoes, inside your skin
and beneath your hair,
on freshly cut grass, a double-decker bus,
or in bed, slipping into a dream.

In a map of your day
you are here, bookmarking
this page, passing ginger biscuits,
dodging umbrellas
as you dash through the rain.

You are blowing on a hot chip
and laughing with a friend.
Breathe in the smell of vinegar
and place your finger on this moment.

You are here! You are here!

TAKE THE LEAP

Blink, breathe in,
hold your pen and begin.
Ready, steady, set? You Bet!

Behind the white line
crouch down, starting gun.
Ready, steady, set? You Bet!

Open the door,
chin up, walk tall.
Ready, steady, set? You Bet!

Centre stage
heart pumps, curtain up.
Ready, steady, set? You Bet!

Measure the cake,
mix the cake, bake.
Ready, steady, set? You Bet!

Count yourself in,
one, two, three, now sing.
Ready, steady, set? You Bet!

Bounce on your feet,
make the run, take the leap.

Ready, steady, set?
You Bet!

WONDER OF THE EVERYDAY

On this day bread was toasted, a hat blew away,
a book was opened, bubblegum snapped,
a new star formed, shirts dried on the line,
a puzzle was solved, a message was sent.

On this day a tree was planted,
a promise was made, tea was stirred,
dust motes danced, a book was lent,
shoes came unlaced, noodles were sucked up
and someone asked, *Is space infinite?*

On this day a black hole was photographed,
an elephant was born, a wellington leaked,
a book was lost, a selfie was taken,
salt was sprinkled, a whale sang.

On this day rain fell, a mountain was climbed,
someone blew a raspberry, a turtle egg hatched,
a hand was held, a book was read,
a dog was hugged and socks were washed.

FOR THOSE WHO DON'T KNOW WHAT TO DO WITH...

A Lake
Tie stars on your pole and fish for wishes,
in its reflection meet your water-twin.
Know it as a child born of ice-age,
catch ripples and wear them in your hair.
Roll up its shine and post it to the Sahara,
keep its secrets secret.
Don't trust its creaking winter skin.
Dip your toe in the Milky Way at midnight,
use its waves to skip with.
Pour its calm in your pocket for a fiery day.

A City

Fold it into an origami boat
so it can visit other countries. Wear its street lights
as jewellery to a party. Take samples of its sounds
and knot them into a song. Brush off the traffic,
then shake it out in fresh air. Let the joy
of its weekends add fizz to your pop.
Use its skyline to comb your hair. Know, by the scent
of toast and jam, that it is Sunday. Wrap it round you
like a blanket to keep you warm.

TWO SPRINGTIME PUZZLES

Compatible Apple

> This tree live-streams sap
> and reboots in spring.
> The birds and bees are browsing.
>
> This tree downloads sun
> and uploads soil. Which apple blossom
> is compatible with sky?
> Blossoms that are pink and white.
>
> Which windfall apples are compatible
> with wasps, cider and pie?
> Granny Smith, Bramley and Williams' Pride.

Springtime Timespring

This rainbud is pink
your rosecoat is warm.

This birthbell is blue
your blueday is soon.

This newdrop is white
your lambs are snowborn.

The eggbirds are hatching
their blackshells outgrown.

MY NAME IS GREY

I fall as fog and rise as smoke,
I bring the night before night's due.
I belong in pigeons, geese and seals.
I am steel.

I am school sweaters and concrete walls
and a battleship at sea. I am soft
as the dust under your bed and rough
as your grandad's beard.

Sketch an elephant, draw its eye
and when you've finished - sign your name.
I am the grey of the pencil
between your finger and thumb.

I am the owl's wing and winter sky,
I leap in the mad March hare.
I hide in the hedgehog's prickles,
and sleep in the wolf's thick fur.

MY NAME IS BLUE

My name is blue. You'll find me
in Van Gogh's starry night
or hiding in the snowy shadows.
I wrapped you up once, after a bath.
Me and stripes of white
– we dried your hair.

In the park you threw me bouncing
to a friend
but barking black-and-brown
leapt up and bit me in half!

Your father sails across me
to other lands and back. Silver and I
are neatly folded round the birthday gift
he wrapped for you. Discover me
in his signed name followed by the x x x.

I am the kingfisher's pride
and the boat's wide sail.
I am your dad's eyes and the jumper sleeve
he wipes them with when I've swallowed
the harbour from sight.

FIRST HAIRCUT

Noises near my ears bring shivers:
a brush of sleeve, the snip of scissors,
my neck feels long and bare.

Something is just behind me:
tiger's whiskers, monkey fingers
or a dragon-claw comb testing my courage.

My legs dangle from a high red chair.
Tufts of hair sparkle as they fall
and the barber's feet shuffle

through red and gold.
It's chilly
where hair no longer grows.

My cape is back to front.
I shut my eyes and feel an eagle's wing
brush both shoulders, then

the cloak is whipped away
and an older-me
stranger meets my gaze.

THE EYES-SHUT
BARBER SHOP

BIRTH DAY

She's no years old, not even a day,
so I bring her a Birth Day gift,
a tin of coloured crayons with a tiger on the lid.
Don't be daft, she's too young, says Mum.

I'm sorry she's toothless and bald,
I'd be crying too.
A Birth Day cake might cheer her up.
Shall I pop and fetch one from the shop?
Don't be daft, she's too young, says Mum.

Wow, now she's really cross.
I'd sing happy Birth Day
but no one's agreed on her name.
Shall we give her the bumps?
Don't be daft, she's too young, says Mum.

Help! A howling sister is in my lap,
what can a big brother as daft as me do?
I bump her up and down, singing,
Happy Birth Day dear baldy,
while rattling the tin of crayons by her ear.
Guess what? The crying stops.
Well done, says Mum. *Well done.*

SOMEONE NEW

Someone was born last night
I stepped outside
where daisies looked up begging me to dance
and opened my arms to pink clouds.

The weight of sky
is bigger than brother-sister
but lighter than the waiting.

It's too soon for daylight
and too late for stars.
My stomach growls
and I spin on wet toes.

Something new has come to us
and the changed air smells of soap and toast.
I wanted to tell the day
so the day could tell the world.

SHE BELONGS TO THE WORLD

Drifting through Albania
from mountain tops to forest floor,
she is *flutur.*

In Estonia,
her wings as bright as stained glass,
she is *liblikas.*

In Norway,
among black pines, a brilliant jewel,
she is *sommerfugl.*

In Italy,
among spring scents and colour,
she is *farfalle.*

Dancing in Spain,
floating closer and closer,
she is *mariposa.*

Resting in France,
basking in the sun,
she is *papillon.*

Sheltering in Ireland,
in green shade and soft rain,
she is *féileacán.*

In Scotland,
where the purple thistles sway,
she is *dealan-dè.*

Dancing through Wales,
winging further and further,
she is *pilipala.*

Tumbling from the sky,
summer has arrived.
She is Butterfly.

PADDLE IN THE PUDDLE OCEAN

In the puddle ocean
are tiny rainbow islands. Swirling
purple islands, blue surf and violet sand.

In the puddle ocean, giants
plod through, dragging giant dogs
who try to drink the sea.

In the puddle ocean, leaf-ships sail,
captained by beetles tidying their wings.
Bright skies are mirrored

in the puddle ocean and spinning
in the ripples are sweet-wrapper ducks
and soda-can submarines.

When the rain has gone and puddles
sparkle in the sun, let's go paddling
in the puddle ocean.

ODE TO A STEPLADDER

We met at a birthday party. I was holding a balloon,
he was propped against a wall.
I like your rungs, I said.

The way he leaned seemed kind and calm.
Old wood spotted with green gloss paint.
I climbed up

and tied the balloon to the top.
He looked pleased, as much as a ladder can,
and we made friends.

My ladder helped me put up shelves
and hang sticky rolls of wallpaper
(yellow roses).

Together, my ladder and I
rescued the cat from the plum tree,
then he stood, never wobbling, while I picked plums.

Today, my old friend rests
in the garden shed,
helping spiders make oblong webs.

THANK YOU, TOES

See this row of toes, wiggle them
and watch them dance
on their little fan of bones.

Thank them for pedalling the pedals
and all the races you won.
Thank them for tiptoeing you to bed
and waltzing you to breakfast in the morning.

Cut their nails kindly.
Cross your legs with bare feet
so your little toes
occasionally get to meet.

Listen to them pleading
for soft socks.
Listen to them begging
you to go to the beach and paddle.

Thank your toes
and they will grow still.
They are listening.
Thank them.

KITTY-CAT STREET

Let's all meet on Beehive Street
where crowds crisscross, lickety-split
buzzing with news of where's best to eat.
Taxi! Take us to Beehive Street.

Let's all meet on Parakeet Street,
preen your feathers, polish your beak.
Who's the brightest, who's the loudest?
Taxi! Take us to Parakeet Street.

Let's all meet on Dolphin Street
where we sing of fish and ships,
salty songs on salty lips.
Taxi! Take us to Dolphin Street.

Let's all meet on Alligator Street
where teeth are sharp and still waters run deep.
Watch your back — be quick on your feet.
Taxi! Take us to Alligator Street.

Let's all meet on Kitty-Cat Street
where the grass is green and the flowers smell sweet,
chase a feather then fall asleep.
Taxi! Take us to Kitty-Cat Street.

DAUGHTER OF FIRE AND WATER

When water met fire she spat like a cat
and stories poured from the old teapot.
Steam, their pale shy daughter,
whispers from ironed shirts,
fogs the kitchen windows
and dances up from the pasta pot.
When fire met water he hissed to a halt
and stories poured from the old teapot.

When water met fire she spat like a cat
and stories poured from the old teapot.
Steam, their determined daughter,
heaps clouds over the cooling towers,
hauls steam engines between
Porthmadog and Ffestiniog.
When fire met water he hissed to a halt
and stories poured from the old teapot.

When water met fire she spat like a cat
and stories poured from the old teapot.
Steam, their wayward daughter,
snakes up from jungle canopy-tops,
she makes New Orleans jazzy
when the summer rain falls hot.
When fire met water he hissed to a halt
and stories poured from the old teapot.

THE TREE THAT SAVED A TOWN

The Tree That Walked swayed along our dusty road,
bringing its shadow along our dusty road.
A giant! The Tree That Walked.

The Tree That Walked did not look around,
it did not rest. Caterpillars swung
from invisible threads and birds fluttered,
but not one egg fell from a nest.

It crossed the highway, the railway, a runway.
A film truck followed The Tree That Walked,
a general offered to blow it up, a politician mentioned
climate talks. Headlines shouted, TREE WALKS!

Up our dusty road it came, rustling past the dusty sign
that read, 'Welcome to Dusty Town.'
A place where dogs' tongues hang out by miles
and the grass is always dry and brown.

But now the fuss has all died down, we rest
in the shade of The Tree That Walked, to watch
the leaves and touch the bark. This morning
we heard the dawn chorus for the first time.

This morning The Tree That Walked
had scattered its seeds. We'll grow
ourselves a forest, we thought, and made
a brand-new sign: 'Welcome to Woodland Town'.

BELONGING STREET

We live at Leaky Roof, This Place.
We brush our teeth
in a washing up bowl
at Leaky Roof, This Place.
None of us sleeps deeply
at Leaky Roof, This Place.

We used to live at
Back Home, the Old Place.
I was born at Back Home, the Old Place.
There was a blue front door,
we had our own beds
and knew the names
of all our neighbours.

Now, my mother and I talk
about Belonging Street.
We invented it one night,
whispering in the dark.
I can't wait. I hope
that you will visit us
when we've moved
to Belonging Street.

COMING HOME TO YOU

Today, I spread my wings then topple
from a clifftop to you.
Over miles of sea foam and tides
I make my way home to you.

Today, I uncurl from my shell and slide
inch by inch to you.
Through a green world of things to chew
I make my way home to you.

Today, I stretch, then race
on all four paws to you.
Through a tail-wagging world of smells
I make my way home to you.

Today, I wriggle from water, then hop
on new legs to you.
Past lilies, herons and willows
I make my way home to you.

Today, I unfold myself to dance
from daisy to daisy to you.
Through gardens of green and white
I make my way home to you.

CITY SEED SONG

I'm going to grow roots,
strike me down some roots,
right here where I lie
I'll put down roots.
No fancy flowerbed,
no butterflies round my head –
here, beneath your boots,
I'm putting down roots.

I'm going to make this city green,
a deep shining green,
right here where I lie
I'll make this city green.
No fancy flowerbed,
no butterflies round my head –
here, between brick walls,
I'm growing wild and green.

I'm going to touch the sky,
grow high as sky,
right here where I lie
I'm growing to the sky.
No fancy flowerbed,
no butterflies round my head –
here, where life rushes by,
I'm reaching for the sky.

NAMING YOUR DAYS

Most days you are
    a kite in the wind
    a bottle full of pop
    a rocket taking off
    a frog full of hop

But some days you are
    a phone with no ring
    a kettle with no steam
    a yo-yo without string
    a plane with one wing

Most days you are
    a castle with bounce
    balloons that rise
    a boat that floats
    a sherbet surprise

But some days you are
    bananas with no yellow
    a hat with no bobble
    a cold wet flannel
    lettesr in a muddel

GOING UP, GOING DOWN

This lift makes us heavy
This lift makes us light
This lift fits eight
This lift has scratched doors
This lift smells a bit
This lift fits two bikes
This lift travels fourteen floors
This lift breaks
This lift works
This lift annoys grandmothers
This lift has seen some sights
This lift takes us home
This lift takes us out
This lift clanks and wobbles
This lift feels different at night
This lift makes friends gossip
This lift makes strangers quiet

SLOW STOPPIES AND HOPS

Watchers high-five my hops,
as tapping the brakes I balance
my weight. In tyre-hissing silence
our shadows spin as we drop.

These empty streets are our stage,
streetlights are spotlights
and foxes watch from behind the bins.
Ideas tingle in hands and feet, can we
can-can? Can we superman?

The cold night air smells of pizza,
and freedom. But here come headlights.
A mean beat rolls from open windows
that are sharp with elbows.
We wheelie as one – and we're gone.

TWO AUTUMNTIME PUZZLES

Whose Brain?

Tap, tap, let us in... Look,
we cut you a nose, now breathe.
We carved out two eyes, now see.
Our orange friend, we carved you
a mouth and teeth, now sing!

We made soup from your insides
and swapped a candle for your brain.
But tonight – take your revenge
and scare us with your wicked grin.

Finally, it's time to bury you
so the compost-worms can feast
on your seeds and skin. Shine on,
our orange friend, see you again
next Halloween.

Autumntime, Timeautumn

Let's pick sweet cobberries,
where spiders weave their blackwebs.

In piles of leaves, the sleepyhog
is a rolled up hedgehead.

We hope November's firefires
and bonworks don't wake her.

HOW TO GET OLDER

Go to bed, wake up, eat beans and drink water.
Grow your legs longer than your trousers.
And breathing, don't forget that!
Dodge trouble, seek answers,
that's how to get older.
Use a calculator to add up
how many hours you spend…
being asleep or swiping a screen.
That's how to get older.
Grow some teeth, lose some teeth,
brush some teeth (did I mention breathing?).
Draw cartoons. Laugh. Laugh. Laugh.
Grow your arms beyond your cuffs.
Share stuff, want stuff, know your carbon footprint.
Forget to wipe your feet.
Be early, be late, make mistakes.
Feel your shoes getting tighter,
watch your parents getting shorter.
That's how to get older. Stare
at a full moon through binoculars.
Blink. Think. Ask a nanna what she knows.
Learn the meaning of your name. Disagree
with a friend. Juggle lemons. Dream. Love
looking forward to things. Ask a million
questions and don't stop learning
how much you've still to learn.
That's how to get older.

THE PAST COMES
IN DIFFERENT LENGTHS

A camera flash away and you're captured in a selfie
in the old days
       the other day
          a laugh away
             a heartbeat.
One year away, a cake away, blowing out the candles
in the old days
       the other day
          a laugh away
             a heartbeat.
A flight away, a rush of wind away, family trees uprooting
in the old days
       the other day
          a laugh away
             a heartbeat.
Dinosaurs away, aeons away, the biggest, big bang
in the old days
       the other day
          a laugh away
             a heartbeat.

TIPTOE

The house has fallen silent,
shadow-creatures are prowling,
tiptoe, tiptoe, tip-tiptoe.

Night falls, an owl calls,
something behind us is growling,
tiptoe, tiptoe, tip-tiptoe.

Our eyes are wide,
we must hide,
tiptoe, tiptoe, tip-tiptoe.

Bent double in the cupboard
we try not to breathe,
tiptoe, tiptoe, tip-tiptoe.

As the cupboard door creaks
our knees go weak,
tiptoe, tiptoe, tip-tiptoe.

How we shriek and how we love
playing hide and seek,
tiptoe, tiptoe, tip-tiptoe.

PHOOEY TO ONE-UPPING

When sister Earth one-ups brother Sky
she boasts of her diamonds.
Whoop-de-do to soggy rainbows, she says.
My gems glow, rain or shine.

When brother Sky one-ups sister Earth
he boasts of Northern Lights.
Horsefeathers to fireworks that fizzle out,
my aurora borealis blazes all night.

When sister Earth one-ups brother Sky
she boasts of her lava.
Bunkum to lightning, she says.
My volcanos are the mother of all fire.

When brother Sky one-ups sister Earth
he boasts of typhoons.
Codswallop to quakes, he says.
My twisters flatten towns.

When sister Earth one-ups brother Sky
she boasts of her oceans.
Fiddle-faddle to your raindrops, she says.
All water is mine.

But when mother Moon one-ups
them both, she blinds brother Sky with beauty
then cools sister Earth with high tides.
Balderdash to bickering, she says.
We need some peace and quiet.

SONG OF THE BEGINNING

We played in the volcano but the volcano erupted.
We played in the lava but we blackened the forests.
We played as silver ash but we blew on the wind.
We played in the wind but we drifted to earth.
We played in the earth but the worms, they ate us.
We played in the worms but the blackbird tugged.
We played in the blackbird but the blackbird sang.
Now we are song – now we are home.

WHAT'S IN A NAME?

Moon

In my name
are the eyes of the owl
and the wheels of my turning.
I am the call of the cow who jumped.
Look on me, in my name
is the ooh of midnight waking.

World

In my name is the what, why and who,
a whirl, a whorl, a while. Almost
word, almost wild, in my name
is the amazed oh of life.
My name is old.

Sun

Speak of me as a day of rest.
In my name is the start of summer
and the upturned smile
of all I warm.
In my name are snaking plumes,
unending heat.
Under my gaze you will burn.

ANIMALS NAME THE CONSTELLATIONS

What's in the stars up above?
asked Sparrow of her brother.
   It's the Egg in the Black Nest,
   the Wing and Feather.
Have they been there long?
Forever my love, forever.

What's in the stars up above?
asked Tadpole of his father.
   It's Silver Spawn in the Black Pond,
   the Lily, Carp and Beaver.
Have they been there long?
Forever my love, forever.

What's in the stars up above?
asked Elephant of his sister.
   It's the Herd in the Black Plain,
   the Tusk, Trunk and River.
Have they been there long?
Forever my love, forever.

What's in the stars up above?
asked the whale of her mother.
   It's the Great Net in the Black Sea,
   the lights of the Hunting Ship.
Have they been there long?
Forever my love,
 dive deep.

GUESS WHO

Not burger, not steak, not veal.
Guess who, guess who…
Grass-Grazer, Herd-Thinker, Moon-Singer.

Not deep fried, not nugget, not roast.
Guess who, guess who…
Soft-Talker, Earth-Pecker, Dawn-Fetcher.

Not bacon, not pie, not ham.
Guess who, guess who…
Tail-Curler, Quick-Trotter, Truffle-Seeker.

Not fingers, not tinned, not battered.
Guess who, guess who…
Shoal-Shaper, Silver-Diver, Sea-Surfer.

Not mutton, not wool, not chop,
Guess who, guess who…
Spring-Leaper, Tail-Waggler, Flock-Caller.

Minced, sliced, hot-pot?
No we're not, no we're not, no we're not!

SPEED UP, SLOW DOWN

Being on a train
is like watching a film on fast-forward
tower block, tower block, bridge, bridge, bus.

Another train flashes by
rocking us with a windy shove
back yard, allotments, fence, fence, rooftops.

Leaving town
we roar through a tunnel
dark, light, field, cow, cow.

Stations are a blur as we munch crisps
at ninety miles an hour
bridge, canal, duck, duck, swan.

Then we're buttoning up our coats
and reaching for our bags
cliffs, sea, cloud, cloud, sun.

Sitting on the beach is like a film in slow motion
herring gull, herring gull,
wave, wave,
ripple.

Sand trickles through our fingers
breathe, breathe,
    shell,
        shell,
            pebble.

DOWN THE PLUGHOLE

He had a bath, tugged the chain
and we never saw Uncle Bob again.

But wherever he's gone and wherever he's been
his ears are scrubbed and his hair is clean.
He took a rubber duck and a bar of soap
(he owes Mum rent, but we still have hope).
Every night we call down the drain,
Uncle Bob, do visit us again.

Mum swears he's somewhere on a ship.
Father swears he's done a flit.
Either way, remember Bob –
don't pull out the plug
while you're in the tub.

FIRST DAY OF TERM

He daydreams of space, wishes he could fly in it
until he reaches the sign that says:
Infinity Ends Here.

But the luminous planets
stuck over his bed
are only a mattress-bounce away.

If his mum's car was a rocket
he would buckle up: *three, two, one... lift off!*
Gravitational forces pressing him

back into the seat
until the Earth is as small
as the coins in his pocket.

Instead, they land in Buckland Street,
where his mum leans across to push the door open.
Hurry up, the bell's gone, she says.

He watches her leave, then spacewalks
the empty playground. *The Eagle has landed,*
he whispers. *Houston, are you receiving?*

THE DERBY MATCH IS LOST AND WON

And what a Derby Match it was –
what a final game.
How the players pulled up their shirts
to wipe away sweat

as the striker kissed his thumb,
touched his heart,
then carried the ball through whistles and catcalls.

And how, when the goalie
punched the ball from its curving path,
half the crowd leapt up
while the rest fell back.

And how Grandad slapped
the arms of his chair so hard dust flew up
as from the street came a roaring, *YES!*
And from next door came a howling, *NO!*

And soon we'll bash mud from our boot studs
and kick through the dry leaves of autumn
until someone finds the ball, lifting it
like a trophy already won.

DOGS IN HANDBAGS

I pretend she's my dog and secretly call her Twinkle.
Get in my bag, Twinkle.
But she won't, she's far too big.
She just smiles with teeth and everything.

Dad says her job is dangerous
but when she's home from work I want her to play.
Wear this pink bow, Twinkle.
But she won't, and she won't wear a pink hat.
She scratches her ears, panting and everything.

She sometimes goes abroad,
doing something with rubble after earthquakes.
When she comes home, I balance dark glasses
on her head. *Pose, Twinkle*, I say.
I give her a bunny-nose filter – ten likes already!

But while I'm not looking, she chews the hat,
breaks the dark glasses and pulls off the pink bow.
Be a good girl, Twinkle, I say. *Be cute.*
But she won't, she won't be cute.
It's super-disappointing how she lies around
making stinky gas, snoring and everything.

TWO INVITATIONS

It is lovely to be asked to lunch.
To wait hungrily at the door after knocking
then step into a home that smells of food.
It is lovely when someone points out where you are to sit
and you rest there politely as things are fetched.
Crusty bread and steaming things, dishes
with lids too hot to touch.
You watch and keep your hands still.
There is talking, some laughing.
Plates are passed, then
a plate comes to you, is placed right in front of you,
between your knife and fork.
It is lovely to be asked to lunch.

***

A boy on a bench eats a pie,
six bites, it's done. He thinks
he eats his lunch alone
but beneath the earth, beneath his feet,
someone digs and snuffles, a mole.
Wasps hover by the rubbish bin
where ants march past, one by one.
On the lake, six loud ducks, two silent swans.
As he brushes off his jacket and heads for home
sparrows peck up the crumbs.
He thinks he eats his lunch alone.

FIND YOU, FIND YOU

Chough, whooper swan, curlew,
kittiwake, chiffchaff, cuckoo,
hear you, hear you, hear you.

Redwing, blackbird, yellowhammer,
snowy owl, greenfinch, goldcrest,
paint you, paint you, paint you.

Turnstone, wagtail, woodpecker,
flycatcher, dipper, shoveler,
what do, what do, what do.

Rock pipit, reed bunting, marsh harrier,
sea eagle, willow warbler, tree sparrow,
find you, find you, find you.

Turtle dove, nightingale, puffin,
linnet, song thrush, merlin,
save you, save you, save you.

CARRY OUR CHILDREN AWAY

Acorn, cherry and beech
stone the earth as if to stir a sleeping friend.
Wake up, birds, wake up, squirrels
and carry our children away.

Sycamore, elder, maple, ash
whisper and shake their leaves.
Wake up, wind
and carry our children away.

Trees rustle, eager for their seeds
to escape their shade
and discover what lies beyond
this path, this street, this wood.

Conker, hazel, chestnut
beg us to pause, to pick up and play.
Wake up, people
and carry our children away.

WATCH OUT FOR THE WHISTLER

He whistles to my giddy ant
he whistles fish and ships,
he whistles to the boys and ghouls
with magic in his lips.

He whistles with his hat and soul
practising day and neat.
Without rhyme or raisin, he whistles
to the birds and beasts.

His whistle is a spanner in the words
and sooner or alligator,
sink or swan,
he'll whistle our world upside-dawn.

The whistling man will whistle us
out of our shoes and sharks.
Truth and pies, white or wrong
beware the whistler's mixed-up song.

FRAGILE

I sometimes spit, I sometimes shake.
I am half asleep and half awake.
Under your feet, but not in the way,
I am not a clock, yet I spin night and day.

I am older than the mountains,
older than the sea,
I am strong yet very fragile –
please take care of me.

I saw the dinosaurs come and go,
saw the pyramids when they were new.
I have seen all your ancestors
and want to see your children's children too.

I am neither man nor woman,
my blood is salty and blue.
I have no mother or father
but I am a mother to you.

HEARING THE EARTH, FEELING THE EARTH

Hush-o-clock
The dawn was so peaceful
we heard the sun stirring
The morning was so tranquil
we heard the sky shining
The afternoon was so hushed
we heard the trees hoping
The dusk was so serene
we heard the dog thinking
The evening was so calm
we heard the stars humming
The night was so still
we heard ourselves dreaming

Storm-o-clock

The dawn was so stormy
we felt the sun steaming
The morning was so thunderous
we felt the sky falling
The afternoon was so windy
we felt the trees praying
The dusk was so cold
we felt the dog shivering
The evening was so wild
we felt the stars hiding
The night was so gusty
we felt ourselves wishing

HELPING HANDS

Grandad's hands are brown
and rough with rust and oil.
Grandma has a green thumb,
potatoes pushing up the soil.

My aunt's hands are pale,
inked with many colours.
My uncle's hands are strong,
dusted with sugar and flour.

My stepdad's hand uncurls
to reveal a coin's bright shine.
My mother's strong hands
sew each stitch in time.

And when any of us fall,
these hands will help us stand,
these mending, baking, making,
lending, helping hands.

BEGINNINGS, A MILLION MIDDLES AND AN END

The robber pulls on his magic cape
and sniffs at the morning air. His instincts are good.
A story arrives on the breeze –
a flock of little white sheep
and a yawning shepherd boy, half asleep.

This is the story's beginning,
a rocky path vanishing over a hill
and a mother waving farewell.
Take care, Joseph, take care.

But the story's middle, in the deep blue woods,
has not yet been told,
and on that path, with his little white sheep,
Joseph still walks, half asleep.

Can you imagine a middle that leads to an end
where Joseph returns without any sheep?
Can you imagine a middle that leads to an end
where Joseph returns with sheep and cape?
Can you imagine a middle that leads to an end
where Joseph and the robber make friends?

A million stories of trees that walk,
dragons that talk, tricks and traps
and magic hats. And in the middle of this
imaginary land is Joseph's mother, hoping
for a happy end.

THE RHYTHM OF SLEEP

slip your toes into sleep
slip your shins into sleep
slip your knees into sleep
breathe soft, breathe deep
slip into sleep

slip your hips into sleep
slip your chest into sleep
slip your shoulders into sleep
breathe soft, breathe deep
slip into sleep

slip your elbows into sleep
slip your hands into sleep
slip your fingers into sleep
breathe soft, breathe deep
slip into sleep

slip your neck into sleep
slip your chin into sleep
slip your lips into sleep
breathe soft, breathe deep
slip into sleep

slip your nose into sleep
slip your eyes into sleep
slip your brain into sleep
breathe soft, breathe deep
slip into sleep

THE CHILDREN'S SONG

The night slides from yawning to yawning
from evening to morning.
The orange of a chicken's eye,
bare feet on a warm path,
a walk to school or a walk to fetch water.
And the colours, the laughing,
the breathing, spins the world around
so the dawn sings, *good morning,*
and the night whispers, *sweet dreams.*

And some of us will leave the ground today,
spinning in a tyre on a knotted rope
or swung onto a hip, and some will work,
some will play, some will read,
while most, not all, will eat.
And the colours, the laughing,
the breathing, spins the world around
so the dawn sings, *good morning,*
and the night whispers, *sweet dreams.*

A few will hear a mother hum a tune
and many will sing songs themselves,
others will fall silent at the roar of planes or trucks
and wonder, and wonder, and wonder.
And the colours, the laughing,
the breathing, spins the world around
so the dawn sings, *good morning,*
and the night whispers, *sweet dreams.*

MANDY COE

Mandy Coe is an acclaimed poet, whose verse for children and adults has featured on BBC radio and television. Her work on teaching poetry has been published by the Times Educational Supplement, Bloomsbury and Cambridge University Press, and she is a Visiting Fellow of the Writing School at Manchester Metropolitan University. She co-authored *Our thoughts are bees: Writers Working with Schools* and her poems can be heard on 'Talking Poetry', BBC Schools Radio and at the Poetry Archive. Her first collection for children, *If You Could See Laughter*, was shortlisted for the CLiPPA Award. Mandy Coe regularly works with children through author visits to schools and festivals. She lives in Liverpool.

www.mandycoe.com